Go outside and play!

Why, indeed...

It was in nature where I felt the most calm and content. But, it wasn't just about being happy outside, it was about the intrigue, the mystery, the sounds and smells of the woods, and what I felt nature could teach me about myself.

— Ryan Hogan

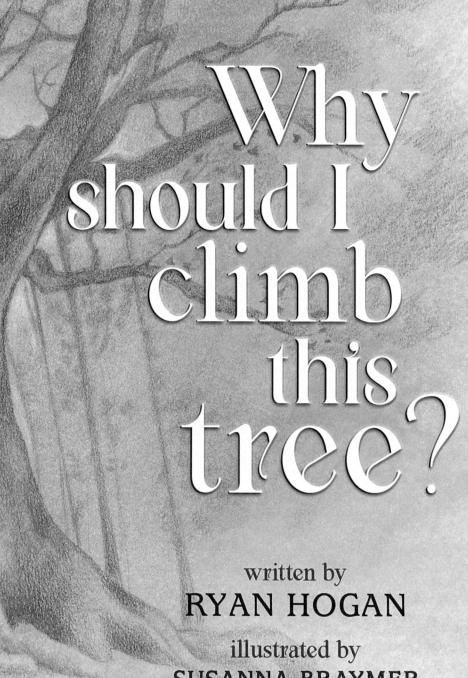

Why should I climb this tree?

written by
RYAN HOGAN

illustrated by
SUSANNA BRAYMER

ILLUSTRATED BY Susanna Braymer | *www.littlepinedesign.com*
BOOK DESIGN BY The Troy Book Makers | Meradith Kill

Printed in the United States of America, *First Edition*

The Troy Book Makers ✳ Troy, New York ✳ thetroybookmakers.com

To order additional copies of this title, contact your favorite local bookstore or visit www.shoptbmbooks.com

ISBN: 978-1-61468-733-7

To Jack

"Why should I climb this tree?"

Said the young boy to me

"There are
many reasons,"
I said,

You never know

what's at the top

Or what you'll learn

along the way

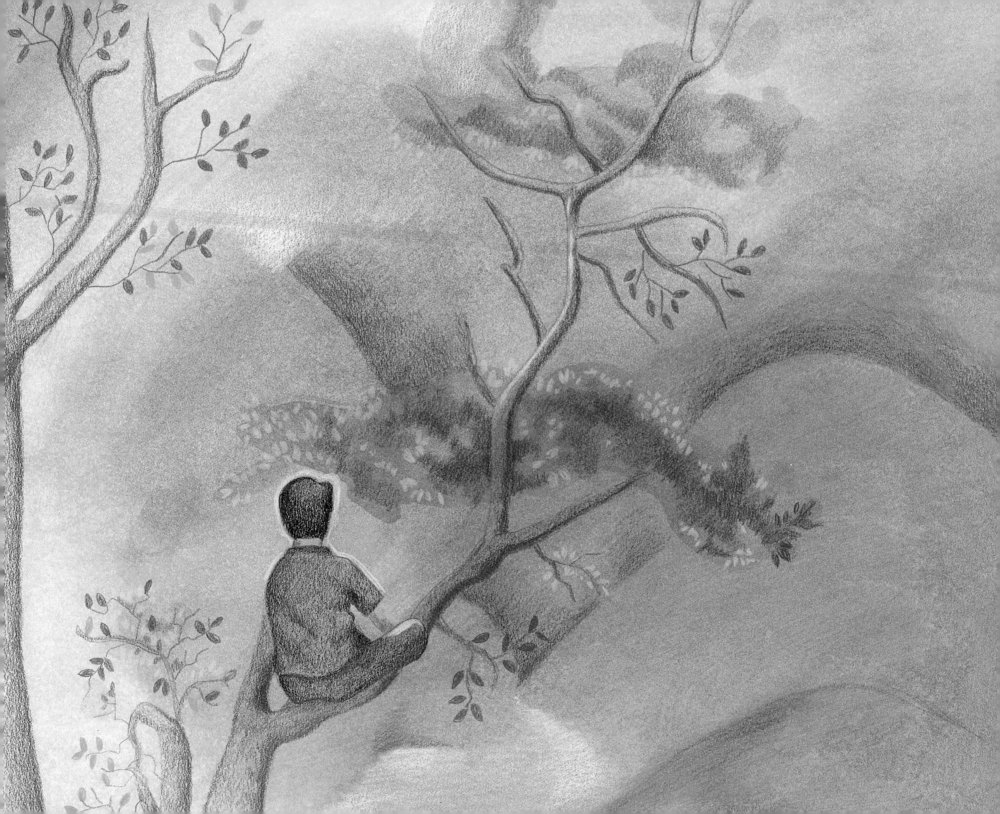

You may decide

to stop,

sit on a branch

and stay

Admire a baby bird

or two in a nest,

who will grow up

to fly someday

The view from the tree top

may inspire you to sing a lovely tune

You know some say

climbing it at night

brings you closer

The feeling you'll get

is sure to set you free

But please wait til it's full

so you can see!

You may discover

something undiscovered,

Or come to know

something unknown

You might just see

something unseen,

Like an animal painting

the leaves green

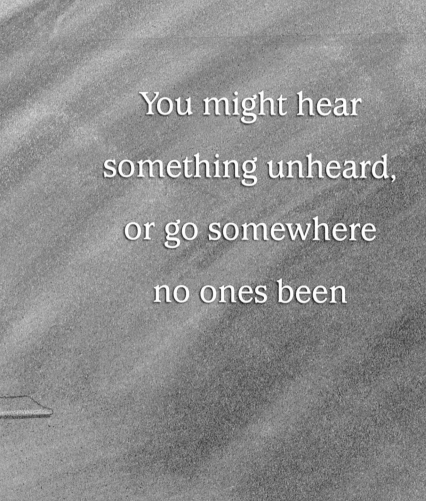

You might hear
something unheard,
or go somewhere
no ones been

Or better yet,

find something

inside yourself that will

surely make you grin

It may be tough

in some spots,

some branches may be

too far to reach,

but I know you'll

make it up,

and return with valuable

lessons to teach

Some trees tell a story.

If you listen close enough

they can tell you how

they grew tall in life,

even when times were tough

Every season has a special beauty

You could be surrounded by pink buds

and red squirrels declaring its Spring

You could feel the Summer breeze

from the top, and with it hear

the distant bells ring

What I love best are all

the colors in the Fall

And remember from that height,

it will be easier to hear

Dad's dinner time call

The world looks different from up high

It will make your troubles seem ok,

you should give it a try

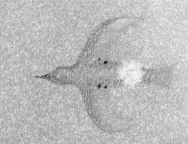

When I was a boy your age,

I climbed that very tree

I went up, up, up in skies blue and grey

And it made me who I am today

Take a deep breath,

one

step

at

a

time

Go ahead and climb it,

and see what you can see

You just might

discover the person

you want to be.

Who am I?

1 Pileated Woodmeleon

2 Arbor Fish

3 Baticoot

4 Duckdeer

5 Lemurfly

6 Peakoala

7 Skabbit

8 Cottontail Dovebunny

* *And don't forget the Mippits!*

1

2

3

4

5

6

7

8

Special Thanks

Special thanks to my Mother, Father, my Brother Matt/companion in the woods, Jack and Alexis, Karen, Farrah, Meg, Brian, Keith, Billy, Joanna, Bonnie, The Navengers, Meradith @ TBM, and 66 Ray. I truly appreciate everyone who contributed their encouragement and belief in this book and idea—to get children back outside again exploring and reveling in this wonderfully colorful world.

 Ryan Hogan

Special thanks to my husband Scott for seeing me through on this project, to Ryan for his partnership, and to my family for their love and support.

Susanna Braymer